BIONICLE®

THE SECRET OF CERTAVUS

BY GREG FARSHTEY

ILLUSTRATED BY
JEREMY BRAZEAL

SCHOLASTIC INC.

NEW YORK   TORONTO   LONDON   AUCKLAND   SYDNEY
MEXICO CITY   NEW DELHI   HONG KONG   BUENOS AIRES

ISBN-13: 978-0-545-09336-1
ISBN-10: 0-545-09336-8

12 11 10 9 8 7 6 5 4 3 2 1   9 10 11 12 13 14/0

Book designed by Cheung Tai and Henry Ng
Printed in the U.S.A.
First printing, March 2009

Gresh stood in the arena. He was wearing armor and carrying a Thormax shooter.

On the other side of the arena stood Tarix. He also wore armor and carried his sword. As the villagers cheered, the contest began.

Tarix struck first, swinging his water sword. Gresh ducked, then he leaped in the air, spun, and swung his Thormax shooter.

But Tarix jumped out of the way and hit Gresh with the flat part of his sword. Gresh fell to the sand.

"I won," said Tarix, smiling.

"This is only practice," Gresh reminded him as he got up. "If it were a real fight, things might be different."

Tarix laughed. "Not with those moves, my friend. I've seen that leap and spin too often. You need some new tricks."

Gresh sat and thought for a long time. Maybe Tarix was right. Maybe he needed a new idea.

Just then Berix called to him.

"Um, excuse me, Gresh?" Berix said. "I heard what Tarix said, and...well, I thought you might want to see this."

Berix handed him a torn piece of very old paper. Written on it was a name—Certavus. Every fighter knew that name. Certavus was famous for his skill.

"This might have come from a scroll or a
book," said Gresh. "Berix, I want you to show me
where you found this!"

They made a deal. Berix would lead Gresh to
the ruins where he found the paper, and in return,
Gresh would stand guard while Berix searched for
more valuable items.

Gresh and Berix began to their long journey. They left the jungle behind and headed across the desert sands. To the north, they could see a chain of high mountains. To the south, there was more sand and the outlines of other villages, far in the distance.

Suddenly Gresh stopped. The sand all around them had started to move, but it wasn't because of the wind.

He and Berix started to run toward some ruins. Behind them, six Vorox rose out of the sand dunes. The Vorox hid in the sands of the wasteland and hunted travelers.

Berix looked over his shoulder. The Vorox were chasing them and they were gaining.

Gresh picked up Berix and threw him over a low wall. The villager landed in the soft sand. "Stay down!" Gresh yelled. "I'll handle them!"

Berix peered over the rock wall. He couldn't believe what he was seeing. Gresh was fighting six Vorox! A few times, Berix was sure Gresh was about to lose. But Gresh always managed to drive the Vorox off.

After many hours, the Vorox pulled back.
Gresh was too tired to go after them. He walked
slowly toward the ruins. Once he was there, he
collapsed on the ground next to Berix.

"They are tough," Gresh said. "I'm not sure I can stop them a second time."

"Then we have to find a way out of here!" said Berix.

Gresh shook his head. "The Vorox are out there, waiting. What we need is some kind of new trick I can use to beat them. We need that book."

Berix scrambled to his feet. "Then let's find it!"
They started searching the ruins. Long ago, this
place had been a training center for fighters. Old
pieces of armor, weapons, and practice dummies
were scattered all over the area.

"So do you really think this book is going to help?" asked Berix.

"It has to," said Gresh. "Certavus was a great fighter. He had to know the secret to winning any battle."

Nearby, Berix had climbed a ruined wall. As he reached the top, he saw six warriors waiting for him. He yelled and started to scramble back down. Then he stopped. They weren't warriors at all, just more practice dummies.

"Wow," Berix said to himself. "If you look quickly, those seem just like the real thing. Hey, Gresh!"

Berix turned and stopped, his mouth open in shock. A Vorox was burrowing its way up through the sand in the center of the ruins. Gresh saw it, too. He charged at the Vorox. It knocked Gresh to the ground with its stinger.

"Hang on! I'm coming!" yelled Berix. He jumped from the top of the wall, but his feet got tangled in the practice dummies. His jump turned into a fall and the dummies fell with him.

The Vorox looked up at Berix and then it did an amazing thing. It dove back into the hole in the sand.

"How do you like that?" Berix said, smiling. "I scared him off!"

"Well, something did," said Gresh. He looked around at the dummies lying on the sand. "But I'm not so sure it was just you. Berix, I think I've been doing things all wrong."

"How do you mean?" asked Berix.

"I've been trying to outfight the Vorox. . .and even Tarix back in the village," said Gresh. "But maybe the answer isn't to be stronger than my opponent. Maybe I just need to be smarter. . .a lot smarter."

Gresh and Berix gathered every practice dummy and all the old armor and swords they could find. Then they propped the dummies up all along the walls and gave them each a mask and a weapon.

When they were done, it looked as if an army was guarding the ruins. "But do you think this will fool the Vorox?" asked Berix.

"If it doesn't," said Gresh, "it will be the last trick either of us ever plays."

The first rays of morning sun lit up the ruins. Beyond the walls, the sand began to shift as the Vorox prepared to attack again.

When the first Vorox emerged, Gresh drew his weapon. "These ruins are ours!" he shouted. "Go away!"

Berix scurried from dummy to dummy, shaking them and waving the swords in their hands. Now and then, he would yell, "That's right!" or "Let's get them!", using different voices each time.

The Vorox started to move toward the ruins. Then they stopped. They were confused. Were those really more fighters, or was it a trick?

First one Vorox, then another and another, began to back away. Berix raced around, making the dummies move all along the walls and shouting. Now all the Vorox were running away!

"We did it!" said Berix.

"We can celebrate later, when we're back in the village," said Gresh. "We better get out of here before they come back."

Berix was running to join Gresh when he noticed something poking out of the rubble. He pulled it out. It was an old, worn copy of a book. On the cover was the name Certavus.

"Gresh!" Berix yelled. "I found it! I found the book—the one on how to win any fight!"

Gresh looked over his shoulder and smiled. "Thanks, my friend. But you know what? I don't think I need it anymore."

Berix flipped open the cover. On the first page, these words were written:

"A fighter's greatest weapon is his mind. The mind is a more powerful weapon than any sword and a more powerful defense than any shield."

Berix smiled and closed the book. Gresh didn't need to read this, after all—in these ruins, he had already learned the secret of Certavus.